# BEANO®

## DENNIS & GNASHER
### THE ABOMINABLE

**I. P. DALEY**
Craig Graham  Mike Stirling

Illustrated by
Nigel Parkinson

First published in Great Britain 2021 by Farshore
An imprint of HarperCollins*Publishers*
1 London Bridge Street, London, SE1 9GF
www.farshore.co.uk

HarperCollins*Publishers*
1st Floor, Watermarque Building, Ringsend Road
Dublin 4, Ireland

Written by I.P Daley, Craig Graham & Mike Stirling
Edited by Thomas McBrien
Illustrated by Nigel Parkinson
Cover Design & Additional Illustration – Ed Stockham
Creative Services Manager - Usha Chauhan
Executive Producer – Rob Glenny
Art direction by Catherine Ellis
Text design by Janene Spencer

BEANO.COM

A Beano Studios Product © DC Thomson Ltd (2021)

ISBN 978 0 7555 0324 7
Printed in Great Britain
001

All rights reserved. No part of this publication may be reproduced,
stored in a retrieval system, or transmitted, in any form or by any
means, electronic, mechanical, photocopying, recording or otherwise,
without the prior permission of the publisher and copyright owner.

Stay safe online. Any website addresses listed in this book are
correct at the time of going to print. However, Farshore is not
responsible for content hosted by third parties. Please be aware that
online content can be subject to change and websites can contain
content that is unsuitable for children. We advise that all children
are supervised when using the internet.

MIX
Paper from
responsible sources
**FSC™ C007454**

FSC
www.fsc.org

This book is produced from independently certified FSC™ paper
to ensure responsible forest management.

For more information visit: www.harpercollins.co.uk/green

# Contents

# Welcome to... BEANOTOWN!

Beanotown Library, Beanotown's tallest building. It has the most stories, you see!

Bash Street School, where all the coolest kids go.

This is where the Menace family lives. Menaces by name, Menaces by nature. At least that's what the neighbours say!

# Chapter One

# WINTER IS COMING

Beanotown. November 30th, 11.59 and 58 seconds PM...

'What was that?' muttered Dennis Menace, sitting up in bed. Gnasher, Dennis's faithful dog and best friend, snored chasing cats in his sleep.

Dennis had definitely heard a **FWUMP!** or maybe even a **FLUMP!** He jumped out of bed and ran to the window.

When he saw the snow, Dennis threw open his window and shouted.

# 'WAHOOOO! SNOW!'

Dennis had reason to be excited. Recently, world-renowned Beanotown scientist Professor Von Screwtop had discovered that Beanotown snow is in fact Superior Snow, which is perfect for making snowballs, slides and snowmen.

**PROFESSOR VON SCREWTOP'S SCIENTIFIC STUDY OF SUPERIOR SNOW**

SQUISH FACTOR – 9.7
MOULDABILITY RATIO – 15:1
SLIDINESS – 11
(10 is the maximum ever measured outside Beanotown)

IT'S ZE APPLIANCE OF SCIENCE!

Thanks, Prof! – Ed.

It's also impossible to drive on Beanotown snow, which means all the cars are stranded ... it's **KID HEAVEN!**

The next morning, Dennis and Gnasher went out early to make the most of it. Dennis was making a snowman when his friends Rubi and Vito arrived.

'Hi!' said Dennis. 'What's happening?'

'Just trying out my new snow tyres,' said Rubi, patting the chunky tyres she'd fitted to her chair.

'**They're epic!**' said Vito. 'They look awesome!'

RUBI VON SCREWTOP

THEY'RE WELL SMART, RUBES!

MARIA VITTORIA

Rubi is Professor Von Screwtop's daughter. They live at Beanotown's Top Secret Research Station. Rubi says she could tell her pals what they do there, but then she'd have to tickle them. She's smart, cheeky and a total science geek (the good kind), and was voted 'Most Likely to Create a Mutant Life Form' by her classmates.

Maria Vittoria – Vito for short – is energetic, fearless and green. That makes her sound like a stunt iguana, but she's not *actually* green, just eco-friendly. Although, if she sees anyone dropping litter, she can be pretty eco-*un*-friendly too!

'Do you guys want to help me build a snowman?' Dennis asked.

When they were finished, they named
it *The Stinker*.

'What now?' asked Dennis.

'Let's build a giant snow slide,' said Rubi.

'On Injury Hill!' added Vito.

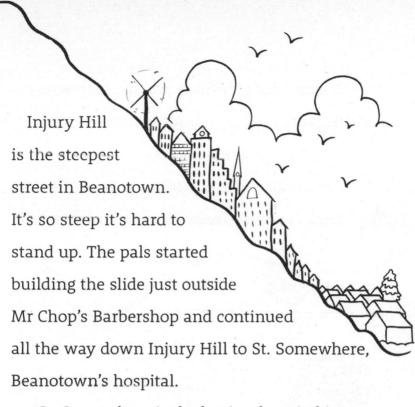

Injury Hill
is the steepest
street in Beanotown.
It's so steep it's hard to
stand up. The pals started
building the slide just outside
Mr Chop's Barbershop and continued
all the way down Injury Hill to St. Somewhere,
Beanotown's hospital.

St. Somewhere is the busiest hospital in
the country. It's a world-leader in treatment of
injuries caused by pianos or bank safes falling
on people's head, mostly because Calamity
James (the unluckiest boy in the world) lives
nearby and this sort of thing happens
to him all the time. They keep

7

a bed ready just for James, and the ladies' toilets on the fourth floor – Felicity's Flushers – are named after his mum.

Just as they were about to try out the slide, Betty arrived. Betty Bhu is in Year 3 at Bash Street School, three years below Dennis and his pals. Her family are from Nepal, and Betty is really proud that her teeny-tiny little country contains the highest mountain in the world, Mount Everest.

'Hi,' she said cheerily. 'Cool slide! Can I have a go?'

It's a rule in Beanotown that you have to ask permission if you want to use a slide that you didn't help to build.

It's also a rule that you never say no if

someone asks to use your slide.

'Sure thing, Betty,' said Dennis, as he stepped onto the slide.

WHOOSH!

Dennis was gone!

'After us!' grinned Rubi, pulling a lever on her chair. Two skis slotted into place beneath her wheels.

Vito took her hand. 'We're going twosies!' she said.

Then THEY were gone!

WHOOSH!

Betty, not wanting to be left behind, jumped onto the slide.

WHOOSH!

The slide was so fast they triggered the
speed camera outside Wiggy Stardust, the
wig-makers shop.

'That was **Snowmazing!**' said Dennis
when they were all at the bottom.

'Let's do it again!' laughed Vito, high-fiving
Rubi.

There was a shriek from the further up
the hill.

'Uh-oh!' said Rubi. 'Betty's coming in fast!'

They watched in horror as the little figure
rocketed down the hill, clipped the kerb and
flew into the air.

WHEEEE!

IS IT A BIRD?

IS IT A PLANE?

NO, IT'S BETTY BHU!

Betty landed head-first in a snowdrift.

**PAFF!**

'Help her!' cried Rubi.

'I can hear her screaming in pain!' cried Vito, as they dug her out.

'She isn't screaming,' said Dennis. 'She's laughing!'

Dennis yanked Betty out of the snow by one ankle.

'Best. Fun. Ever!' said Betty.

'You shouldn't have gone so fast,' said Rubi, crossly. 'You might have got hurt in the snow.'

'I love the snow,' said Betty. 'You should see the snow my grandma's village in Nepal gets. It's way above my–'

'Look out!' shouted Vito. 'We've got another slider!'

Moments later another man did the same, only less gracefully.

'I don't think they enjoyed the slide much,' said Rubi.

'Serves them right!' said Dennis. 'They didn't ask for a shot of our slide!'

'I don't think they're using the slide on purpose,' said Vito, as a woman hurtled overhead doing the doggy-paddle. Maybe she thought she could fly to work.

> You've got to give her points
> for trying! – Ed.

'We have to do something,' said Vito.

'Someone's going to get hurt.'

Dennis started to trample the snow

beneath his feet.

COME ON! HELP ME MAKE THE SLIDE LONGER!

'How will that help?' asked Betty.

They shuffled, stamped, scraped and shaped the snow until Dennis was satisfied.

'There!' he said. 'Now the slide takes them straight to the doors of A&E, so if they do pick up a bruise or two, they can get help.'

They all stepped back as a very unhappy-looking man slithered past on his bottom, finally stopping at the end of a queue of grumpy adults rubbing their bruised heads, arms and legs.

'They still don't look very happy,' said Betty.
Dennis couldn't believe it, but Betty was
right. The grown-ups really
did look pretty grumpy.
'See you later,' said
Betty, heading back
up Injury Hill to her
house. 'I only came out
to buy some milk for
my mum.'

SOME PEOPLE ARE
NEVER HAPPY!

'Let's go to
the den,' said
Vito. 'We've still got time
for a snowball fight before school.'
'I'll text Minnie,' said Rubi. 'She'll be cross
if we don't invite her.'

# Chapter Two

# INTO THE WOODS

Dennis is really lucky. He has two dens.

One is his tree house in the garden at
51 Gasworks Road.

THAT'S WHERE I LIVE. I DON'T HAVE A TREE HOUSE IN SOMEBODY ELSE'S TREE. THAT WOULD JUST BE WEIRD.

He also has another den in Beanotown
Woods. The den in the woods
is much bigger and completely
awesome. Dennis built it with his friends
so they could hang out somewhere far
away from any groan-ups.

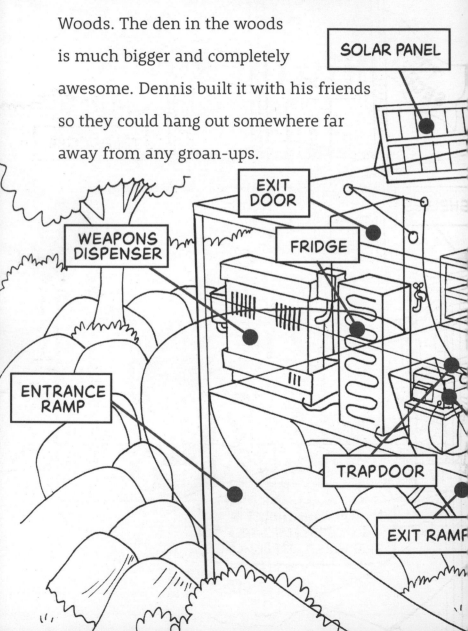

SOLAR PANEL

EXIT DOOR

WEAPONS DISPENSER

FRIDGE

ENTRANCE RAMP

TRAPDOOR

EXIT RAMP

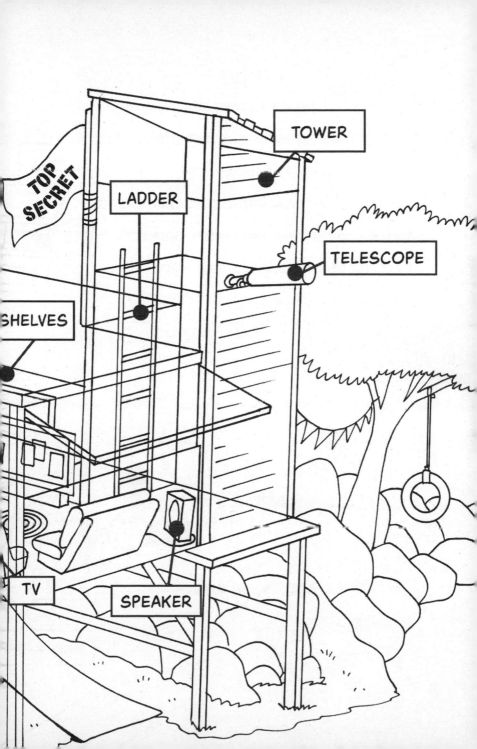

When they got to the den, however, it wasn't quite as awesome as usual. In fact, it was completely trashed!

'O.M.G.!' said Dennis. 'What happened here?'

'The roof's buckled!' said Rubi.

'The door's hanging off!' said Vito.

'And it STINKS!' said Dennis, holding his nose.

Dennis crept a little closer and peered through the door.

'It's okay,' he said. 'There's no one in here.'

Vito climbed through the door. 'Going by the smell, I'd say a wild animal did it.'

'It's nothing we can't fix,' said Rubi, checking out the damage.

'It's weird, though,' said Dennis. 'If it was an animal, it would have to be a really BIG–'

He stopped and let out a wail. He pointed at the drawer where their sweetie stash was usually hidden. The drawer was empty.

'All gone!' groaned Dennis. 'Everything except the Red Hot Chilli Gobstoppers.'

WHYYYYYYYYY?!

Vito examined a wet, sticky, red ball which was half-buried in the wall. Gnasher gave it a sniff, then decided not to lick it.

'Looks like our thief tried a gobstopper, then spat it out at a hundred miles an hour!' said Vito.

'Who would do such a thing?' wailed Dennis.

'Hmmm,' said Rubi. 'We could probably get DNA from the mucus on the gobstopper and find out who did it.'

'We're looking for a criminal who drools a lot . . .' said Dennis, grimly.

'. . . And who has a really, really sweet tooth,' added Vito.

'. . . And they smell really, really bad,' finished Dennis.

'Good work, Sherlock,' said Rubi. 'That narrows it down to every teacher in the country!'

'We could start with the usual suspects,' suggested Vito.

Vito slowly made her way to the back

of the den, looking down at the floor as she went. She spotted some strange marks in the ground . . .

'There's a very faint trail,' she said. 'There are damp patches all *down the ramp!*'

USUAL BEANOTOWN SUSPECTS

DENNIS'S DAD

RASHER THE PIG

'Izz it juzzt me,' said Rubi, holding her nose, 'or izz de smell gedding worze?'

'Sorry,' chuckled Dennis. 'That was me!'

'Stop joking around!' Rubi whispered. 'What if the dastardly den-destroyer is hiding down here?'

Vito stopped.

'If it were here, we'd be able to see it,' said Vito. 'Look!'

'I can't look!' said Dennis. 'The smell
is making my eyes water!'

'O.M.G.' said Rubi, ignoring him. 'I've
never seen anything like it!'

Dennis looked down at the footprint.

It was big.

PHEW! I'VE NEVER
SMELLED ANYTHING
LIKE IT EITHER!

# REALLY BIG!

Dennis put his foot inside it to compare the size.

Gnasher whimpered.

'It's okay, Gnasher,' Dennis said, rubbing his dog's head. 'I won't let anything hurt you.'

'It's unbelievable,' said Rubi. 'There's no creature on this planet big enough to make these footprints!'

'Well,' said Vito. 'Nothing we *know* about!'

Now you've put your foot in it, Dennis! – Ed.

27

The **giant footprints** led away from the den and into the undergrowth.

'Whatever it is,' said Rubi, 'it went that way.'

They froze, afraid to move a muscle. Dennis tried not to think, in case whatever-it-was could read minds.

There was something in the bushes.

*Behind* them.

## Chapter Three

# IT WENT THAT-A-WAY

'BOO!' said a voice behind them.

'MINNIE!' gasped Vito. 'You nearly gave us a heart attack!'

Minnie was already kneeling on the ground, looking at the tracks left by the den's night-time visitor.

'Look!' she said. 'I found a giant stinky footprint.'

Minnie is Dennis's cousin. They're the same age, but Minnie thinks she's Dennis's superior in every way except stuff she doesn't like. Their relationship kind of works. As long as Dennis doesn't argue.

'Correction,' said Dennis, forgetting not to argue. '**We** found a giant stinky footprint,'

'Oh, really?' scoffed Minnie. 'So why haven't you tracked down the massive mystery monster yet? Huh?'

'Well, we only just found it,' said Dennis, weakly.

'It went that way,' said Minnie, pointing at a trail of prints leading into the bushes. 'Follow me, and no more excuses!'

*Excuses?* thought Dennis, as he followed Minnie. **EXCUSES?!**

He was so angry he could feel the blood pounding in his veins!

> The Numskulls are the little people in your head. Everybody's got them. This is what happens when you get so angry you can feel the blood pounding in your veins.

THIS TANTRUM IS IN VEIN!

The den-destroyer was a fast mover. They tracked the giant footprints all around Beanotown.

'Look!' said Vito, as they passed the Town Hall. 'It stood on the empty statue plinth!'

No one can remember whose statue is supposed to be on the plinth, but everyone has a theory.

Sometimes Vito thinks

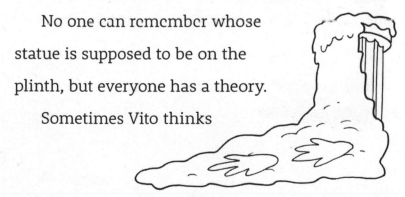

it might have been a statue of something cool, like an extinct species.

Rubi hopes it was a statue to her heroes, the women scientists who have made so many amazing discoveries.

Minnie thinks they're keeping the plinth for a statue of her. Natch!

Dennis likes to stand on the plinth and howl like a wolf: **'AWOOOOOOO!'**

Next, the tracks led them past the skate park.

'It had a go on the half-pipe,' said Dennis. 'Maybe this giant, drooly, stinky-footed monster is cool?'

I pee on the plinth. Gnee-hee!

Things took a turn for the worse when the footprints took a sharp right through the gates of Bash Street School and into the playground.

'Now I'm scared,' said Dennis.

'You're right,' said Vito. 'It might be lying in wait to gobble up some poor, unsuspecting school kids!'

'Or the janitor,' said Minnie. 'There's more eating on a janitor. If I were a monster, I'd hunt down the janitor.'

'No,' said Dennis. 'I'm scared because it went to school when it didn't have to. WEIRDO!'

The footprints curved around to the right, past Class 1A, the swimming pool and the gym.

As the friends skirted the back of the assembly hall, disgusting noises reached their ears. Rubi raised a finger to shush them.

'Hear that? It's eating the janitor!' said Minnie, excitedly. 'Let me see!'

Minnie was wrong. Which is good, because if the monster had been eating the janitor, this book would have been too gruesome to print.

They peered round the corner.

## GROSS!

'Ugh! Is that sprout and gravy trifle?' said Dennis, feeling queasy. 'With curry custard and broccoli ice cream?'

Now Vito actually was green. They ducked back around the corner, out of sight.

'What now?' asked Dennis.

'We need to track it,' said Rubi. 'So we can learn all about it. Where it lives, what it eats, when it poops . . .'

*If it's eating Olive's school dinners, it'll be pooping pretty soon,* thought Dennis.

'No way!' said Vito. 'We need to hide it and help it get back home! It's too big to live in town – there's no such thing as an urban snowman!'

'Personally,' interrupted Minnie, 'I don't care what we do with it as long as it's on my team in this snowball fight we're SUPPOSED to be having!'

'What do you think, Dennis?' asked Rubi. 'Got any better ideas?'

But Dennis wasn't there.

## Chapter Four

# WE COME IN PIECES

Dennis never waits for a better idea. He
generally goes with the first one he has.

He really wanted to meet an abominable
snowman, and that's what he was going to
do. Simples!

Gnasher didn't really want to meet it,
but he wasn't letting Dennis out of his sight.

'Hi!' said Dennis to the creature,
who was delving into Olive's
food slops again.

The snowman turned, surprised, and stared at Dennis. Then, thinking Dennis wanted to share its food . . .

'Ugh!' cried Dennis. 'I didn't want kipper quiche on Tuesday and I want it even less now!'

The snowman shrugged, as if to say 'your loss', then popped what was left of the quiche into its massive mouth.

'What's your name?' Dennis asked. No reply.

'I'm gonna call you Biggy Smells,' said Dennis.

The snowman held out a chilli pepper stuffed with something green and suspicious. One of Olive's Jellopeno Peppers – a hot pepper stuffed with lime marmalade. Dennis shook his head.

'You try, Gnasher,' said Dennis. 'Tell it we come in peace or something.'

**'Gnash-gnash-gnashy-gnash!'** said Gnasher.

**'Uh?'** said Biggy Smells.

'Why is my cousin so useless?' said Minnie in disgust, bending down to scoop up a handful of snow.

'I wouldn't say he's doing badly,' said Rubi. 'He hasn't been eaten yet.'

Minnie patted the snowball into shape

and drew back her arm.

'What are you doing?' cried Vito, horrified.

'Just encouraging Dennis to get a move on,
said Minnie, unleashing her snowball.

It flew across the playground, passed
narrowly over Dennis's head and hit the
snowman on the nose.

TAKE THIS!

WHOOPS!

The snowman looked over to where the snowball had come from. Vito waved sheepishly. Minnie pointed at Rubi.

The snowman bent down and before you could say 'this is an awesome turn-up for the books', unleashed six perfect snowballs at them.

'You missed me!' cried Rubi.

'Missed me too!' laughed Vito.

'Mmmffle!' said Minnie through a faceful of snow. The creature hadn't missed *her*.

'He wants to play!' cried Dennis, scooping up a snowball in each hand and zinging them at Rubi and Vito.

'Who says they're a he?' shouted Vito. 'That's a bit presumptuous, Dennis!'

'Oh yeah!' said Dennis, stopping. 'I just thought a snow-MAN would be a he, you know?'

'Sorry, pal!' he said to Biggy, who was launching snowballs at an incredible rate, literally NEVER missing. 'I'll call you a SnowMENACE from now on, okay?'

'This isn't fair!' yelled Minnie, building a snow-wall to hide behind. 'I wanted the abominable snowmenace on MY team!'

It actually was a bit unfair. The snowmenace was a snowball machine.

They could do skimmers . . .

. . . curveballs . . .

. . . boomerangs . . .

. . . even loop-de-loops!

The snowmenace was so good that eventually Dennis switched sides to make it a fair fight. All of them versus the snowmenace.

It was the most epic snowball fight in history*, although it was a bit one-sided.

*According to *The Most Epic Snowball Fights In History,* written by Willis Butt-Freeze, illustrated by Sir Tunly-Will. Available at Beanotown Library, if you ask Mrs Binding the Librarian extra nicely.

The snowmenace had been building a ledge of snow over their heads. With one last double-sized snowball, the ledge came falling down, burying them deep in snow.

## SPLAFF!!!

'You're the best!' said Dennis when the snowmenace pulled them out of the mini-avalanche. 'The best of all time!'

'Meh, they got lucky,' said Minnie.

'You're amazing,' Rubi said, looking the snowmenace up and down admiringly. 'Where are you from?'

The snowmenace pointed at the very peak of far-off Mount Beano.

'And *what* are you?' asked Vito.

'They're an abominable snowmenace, stupid!' said Minnie.

THUNK!

'Ooh! They didn't like being called that,' said Rubi.

'No wonder,' said Vito. 'Would **YOU** like to be called abominable?'

'**Meh**, I've been called worse,' said Dennis. 'I think Biggy Smells kind of suits them, and it's also the truth.'

'Er, guys?' said Rubi, looking at her smartwatch. 'It's almost nine. We'd better get Biggy out of here before—'

**DRIIING!**

'. . . that,' said Rubi.

A babble of excited voices erupted and grew louder. The pupils of Bash Street School were heading towards them.

Biggy took a step backwards. They looked afraid.

'Don't worry,' yelled Dennis. 'I've got this!'

He grabbed Biggy by the wrist and led them to the school doors.

'What is he doing?' wondered Minnie. 'I *know* he isn't thinking about taking that great big hairy beast into the school.'

Dennis took the great big hairy beast into the school.

'Result!' said Minnie. 'This means guaranteed fun, and none of it is technically my fault.'

## Chapter Five

# HANGING WITH THE BIG KID

The school was quiet. For now, at least.

'You be lookout, Gnasher,' said Dennis.
Gnasher wagged his tail and went on ahead.
Dennis and Biggy tiptoed after him
as quickly as they dared.

They hurried along the
main corridor, Gnasher pausing
to check each doorway before
scurrying past.

One final check at the
corner and Gnasher waved
them up the stairs.

*All clear? Sweet.*

Around to the right, and they were almost

there . . .

**Oh gno! Someone is coming! It's
Winston the Bash Street School cat!**

*Good work, Gnasher*, thought Dennis.

Dennis's classroom – Class 3C – was in

sight. But what if Miss Mistry was already

at her desk? If she saw Gnasher it would be

double trouble. Moving quickly, Dennis walked into the classroom acting normal.

'Sorry I'm late, Miss . . .' Dennis started to say. When he saw Miss Mistry wasn't there, he turned back and gave the signal for Biggy and Gnasher to follow him.

*That's a stroke of luck. Must be karma for all my good behaviour*, thought Dennis.

'You can sit at the back next to me,' said Dennis, pointing Biggy towards the desk furthest away from Miss Mistry's.

Biggy walked over and sat down.

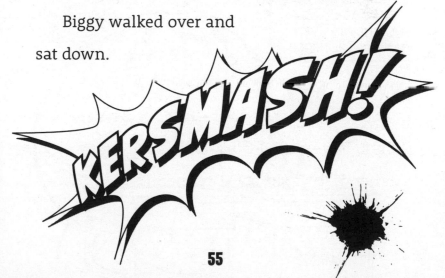

The desk disintegrated under his weight.

'Eek!' said Dennis. 'Grab the smellotape, Gnasher!'

Dennis 'repaired' the splintered desk with a couple of strips of funny-smelling sticky tape, then decided it would be better to just swap it for Walter's. Walter is Dennis's worst enemy. He's a sneak, a tell-tale and a bully. Oh, and his dad is the mayor of Beanotown. But he'll tell you that himself.

The corridor was getting noisy as the rest
of the class approached. Rubi, Minnie and Vito
wandered in, not sure what to expect. Walter
followed, his nose in the air as always. Walter
thought he was better than everyone else at
Bash Street School. When he got to his desk,
though, the smugness dropped away.

'Where's Biggy?' whispered
Minnie, looking all
around her.

'Right there,'
Dennis grinned, pointing.
Biggy waved at Minnie from
behind the maths book.

MY DESK! WHO DID
THIS TO MY DESK?

'I was being sarcastic,
doofus!' snorted Minnie. 'You are in so much
trouble when Miss Mistry gets here!'

But Miss Mistry didn't get there. Instead, at five past nine, Mrs Creecher strode in. Mrs Creecher is the headteacher of Bash Street School. She's Scottish, and she doesn't stand for any nonsense. Luckily, she's a little short-sighted . . .

. . . and didn't notice the gigantic hairy creature sitting in the corner.

'Sit down, Walter' said Mrs Creecher. 'Don't just stand there like a **Soor ploom!**'\*

\*A 'soor ploom' is a retro Scottish boiled sweet which is a bit sour – knowledgeable Ed.

Walter sat down gingerly behind his shattered desk, which promptly collapsed again.

'Walter, you really are a noisy

**KERSMASH!**

**wee bauchle!**'* said Mrs Creecher. She turned her attention to the rest of the class.

'Miss Mistry has been held up by the snow,' she said.

'**HOORAY!**' cheered the class.

'She'll be here as soon as her wee legs will carry her,' continued Mrs Creecher, 'but in the meantime I have some tasks I need help with. The playground needs to be cleared of snow, Olive the dinner lady needs help to clean

*I think it means 'pain in the neck' – not-quite-so knowledgeable Ed.

out her freezer, and Mr Janitor has a delivery
he needs taken to the pool. Are there any
volunteers?'

Five hands shot up into the air. It was
the perfect excuse to get Biggy out of the
classroom.

'What now?' asked Dennis, in the corridor.
'I've never volunteered for anything before!'

'Well, it got us out of the classroom,' said

Rubi, 'but now we have to hide Biggy *and* do all the work!'

'There's a lot of snow to clear,' said Vito, looking out of the window.

Everyone knows the quickest way to clear snow is to make a snowman. With a real snowmenace's help, the gang would be able to build something truly epic!

Gosh! The dog as big as a school? That sounds like the title of a great book! – Ed.

When the playground was clear of snow,
the gang went to the dinner hall to help
Olive clean out her freezer. There was no one
around, but the freezer door was open.
Dennis looked inside and beckoned the others
to follow.

'Hello?' he said.

# HELLO?
## HELLO?
### HELLO?
#### HELLO?
##### HELLO?

'Bit of an echo,' said Rubi.

'No wonder,' said Vito. 'Look at the size of
this place!'

Suddenly, a shaggy, shadowy figure loomed at them through the gloom. Gnasher growled at it, daring it to come closer.

'Sorry kids!' Olive said cheerily. 'I have to suit up to come in here, in case I get lost. Like the last dinner lady . . .'

She paused, as if remembering some great tragedy from a long time ago.

'. . . Anyway, you've come to help me, right?' she continued. 'All the food in here has to go as it's past its use-by date . . . by fifteen years.'

She laughed. 'Call me wasteful, call me

over cautious, but I think it's time it went in the bin.'

'I'll leave you to it. My healthy option oranges won't deep-fry themselves!'

And with that, Olive the abominable dinner lady pounded off to her kitchen.

Biggy was digging through the boxes in the freezer, sniffing each one. Yanking a carton of Stinky Feet ice lollies from the bottom of the pile, it tipped the lollies onto the freezer floor.

Minnie examined the box.

'Best before end of March 1974.' she said.

BIGGY THINKS THEY'RE OKAY!

'Biggy's loving it in here,' said Dennis. 'It's like the Costa del Sol for them!

'Brr!' said Rubi, hugging herself. 'It's not much fun for the rest of us, is it? Let's get on with binning this muck and get warmed up.'

When they'd finished emptying out the stale food, they dragged Biggy out of the freezer. Time to help Mr Janitor.

Mr Janitor had left a trolley outside his office in the basement. It was loaded with boxes of verucca socks and swimming caps for the pool, and bubble bath to go to the janitor's office. The janitor and Winston are big fans of bubble bath.

Biggy carried the supplies to the pool while Rubi powered her pals along at top speed on the trolley.

When they got to the pool, Rubi looked for the shelf where the socks and caps should be stored away.

'Let's see . . .' she said, reading the labels on the storage shelves. '*Va-Va-Verucca, I Can't Believe It Kills Germs . . . Splash and the Germs Are Gone . . .*'

Dennis tapped her on the arm. 'Er, Rubi? We've got a problem.'

Biggy was emptying the last bottle of Mr Janitor's Extra-Bubbly Bubble Bath into the pool.

'**Ooh!**' said Rubi. 'That's 47 times too much bubble bath for a pool this size!'

'What does that mean?' asked Vito.

'Dunno,' said Rubi, happily. 'That's the cool thing about experiments. You try new things and learn something every time!'

They backed away from the rising tide of bubbles (which smelled of peaches) and hurried out of the pool, through

I THINK IT'S TIME WE GOT OUT OF HERE, GANG! SOMETHING'S HAPPENING IN THE POOL!

the changing rooms and into the corridor. As they firmly closed the doors behind them, they met Mr Janitor and Winston. Winston looked at Gnasher suspiciously.

'Sorry I've been a while, kids!' said Mr Janitor. 'Had a vomit-astrophe to deal with in Class 2B. Now, where are those supplies?'

'We put them . . . er . . . in there for you, so you really don't need to go in,' said Dennis. 'Ever!'

'Well, the bubbles are for Winston and I,' beamed the janitor, 'so I'll just grab those and take them down to my . . .'

But the kids were already running down the corridor. *Desperate to get back to their studies,* thought Mr Janitor, foolishly.

He opened the doors to the pool and . . .

It was Mandi Sharma who first noticed the
water in the school corridor. She thought she
should mention it to Mrs Yodel, the school
secretary, but she was a bit worried Mrs Yodel
might be busy. The water was already up to
her ankles when she decided she really had
to tell someone. She splished her way to
the office.

'Hi, Mrs Yodel,' Mandi said. 'Have you noticed that the water level is rising?'

'I hadn't, Mandi,' said Mrs Yodel. 'But if it is rising, I'm sure there's a completely natural explanation for it. If not, Mr Janitor will sort it out. Now you run along and get back to class.'

*Typical groan-up*, thought Mandi, as she splashed along the corridor. The water was up to her knees now. *They never listen!*

THERE'LL BE A BASH STREET SCHOOL OF *FISH* SOON!

Outside the office, Rubi was getting worried. 'Biggy doesn't look too good,' she whispered to Dennis. She was right. Biggy was sweating and looked really grumpy.

'There's definitely something wrong with them,' Rubi whispered to Dennis.

'What's that,
Gnasher?' Vito asked.
'Maybe Biggy's
used to the colder
temperatures outside and the heating
in the school is making him too hot?'

'I've got an idea,' said Rubi, grinning.

She led them back to Olive's giant freezer.

'We've already cleaned out the freezer,
Rubi,' complained Minnie.

Rubi ignored her and showed Biggy two
pipes that led into the freezer.

'See these pipes, Biggy? Can you break them
and stick them in the water?'

Biggy broke the pipes easily and shoved the open ends into the water.

Slowly at first, but then faster, the water started to freeze. Soon the ice had spread right down the corridor.

'Those are the pipes that carry the freezer's refrigerant,' said Rubi. 'You know, the chemical that freezes stuff.'

'You can't fool us with your so-called **fake SCIENCE**, Rubi,' said Minnie. 'We all know it's magic.'

Soon the whole ground floor of Bash Street School was one big ice rink.

This was great for Biggy, who was much happier when it was cold.

ICE, ICE BIGGY! – Ed.

It wasn't so good for the teachers.

'It's break time!' said Dennis. 'We need to hide Biggy before the corridor is full of pesky teachers and 250 kids!'

## Chapter Six

# THE GREATEST ESCAPE

They dashed back to Olive's bins, where they knew no one would willingly come near, because of the smell.

'I don't want to worry anybody,' said Rubi, swiping up on her tablet, 'but my news feed is going crazy. Biggy's footprints have been discovered and EVERYONE is heading for the school right now!'

'**Woo-hoo**! An ice cream van!' said
Dennis, punching the air.

'Is it really bad if Biggy is found?' asked
Minnie. 'Won't they be famous? Imagine how
many followers they'd have if they had their
own Tooter account?'

'They've already got followers, Minnie!' said
Vito. 'The mayor, the police and the media!'

'Don't forget the ice cream van,' said Dennis.

'What do you think will happen if Biggy
is found?' asked Vito. 'Remember the talk the
mayor gave us last year?'

'The one about making sure your vest
always matches your underpants in case you
have an accident?'

'No,' said Vito. 'The one about hunting,
when he told us about all the different animals

he'd like to hang on his study wall!'

'Oh yeah!' said Dennis, feeling his neck.

'One of them was me, wasn't it?'

WHASSUP, DEN?

JUST HANGIN' OUT...

'And then there's Dr Pfooflepfeffer*,' said Rubi.

Dr Pfooflepfeffer is the chief scientist at WilburCorp, officially Beanotown's Most Polluting Company of 2021. She's also one of the governors of Bash Street School! Gulp!

'She'd want to do experiments on Biggy's DNA,' said Vito, 'so she could create super-strong bionic babysitters or something!'

*Puh–foo–ful–puh–feffer – helpful Ed.

The school bell rang four times, meaning everyone was to go to the assembly hall immediately. After leaving Biggy happily munching through Olive's slops again, the gang made their way to the auditorium. Standing on the stage were the mayor of Beanotown and Walter's dad, Wilbur Brown, Dr Pfooflepfeffer and Sergeant Slipper of the BTPD (as he likes to call it) or the Beanotown Police (as everyone else calls it).

'Quiet, boys and girls!' said the mayor.
'Please don't speak, this is your mayor
panicking. Er, I mean, please don't panic, this
is your mayor speaking.'

'Today some HUGE SCARY MONSTER
FOOTPRINTS were discovered in Beanotown,
and we believe the HUGE SCARY MONSTER is
hiding somewhere in this school. This is what
we think the HUGE SCARY MONSTER looks
like . . .'

'. . . and we're getting news reports of a massive increase in injured citizens reporting to the hospital!'

CASUALTY

LET ME GUESS...
YOU FELL DOWN
INJURY HILL?

'The monster didn't hurt those people,' whispered Dennis to his friends. 'Our slide did!'

'Now there's no need to panic,' said the Mayor, 'because I'm PERSONALLY going to catch the huge scary monster.'

'If I don't catch it first,' said Dr Pfooflepfeffer, butting in.

The mayor sighed. Walter had his hand up. 'Yes, Walter?'

'Can we hang its head on your study wall? In the space next to the wild boar?' asked Walter.

'Be quiet, Walter,' said the Mayor, glaring at him. That space was reserved for Dennis.

'Yes, Daddy,' said Walter. 'Sorry, Daddy.'

Dr Pfooflepfeffer stepped forward again. 'A much kinder thing would be to let the beast live at WilburCorp headquarters where it could help us with our completely harmless genetic experiments.'

The mayor glared at Dr Pfooflepfeffer now. If he'd known

IT'S MY MONSTER!

he was going to have to glare so much today he'd have put his glaring glasses on.

'Dr Pfooflepfeffer and I will discuss this and decide that I was right all along,' said the mayor through gritted teeth. 'For now, all of you can go back to your classes, lock the doors, hide under your desks, shut your ears and put your fingers in your eyes. I mean, shut your eyes and put your fingers in your ears.'

As they left the hall, Dennis was grim-faced.

'We can't let them capture Biggy Smells,' he said. 'It was us who let them into the school, after all.'

I THINK YOU'LL FIND IT'S MINE!

'Actually, it was YOU,' said Minnie. Dennis sighed.

'You're right, and I'm going to get them out of here. I just need a plan.'

Dennis stroked his chin, which he'd heard was good for coming up with plans.

Hang on! So the chin–stroking thing actually works! I'm going to try that! – Ed.

GOT IT!

Two minutes later . . .

YOUR PLAN IS A LUNCH TRAY?

YES!

YOU ARE ALWAYS THINKING ABOUT YOUR STOMACH!

Dennis laid the tray on the ground.

'Hear me out,' he said. 'Biggy, lie down on the tray. Now, everyone else gather around.'

Dennis knew his plan would work.

'If we can slide Biggy all the way down to the basement, we can escape through the ancient secret tunnels under the school!'

'Great plan!' said Vito. 'Let's go!'

## ED'S NOTE:

You might be thinking: Hang on! WHAT ancient secret tunnels under the school? If you are, then you probably haven't read *The Battle for Bash Street School* (you should read it, because it's epic),

Anyway, hidden below Bash Street School is a maze of secret, ancient tunnels. No one knows exactly how old these tunnels are or what they were used for, but they're full of booby traps, including hungry, angry crocodiles, massive chewing gum balls and enormous stone slabs of homework. Oh and Dennis's Viking ancestors.

Told you it was epic! Now, back to the story ...

The gang made their way through the school to the basement. Dennis's plan worked beautifully. All they had to do was act innocently whenever a teacher came near.

JINGS! I HOPE THERE'S NO ONE IN THE TEACHERS' TOILET ON THIS FLOOR!

When they got to the basement stairs, Rubi turned her chair in the direction of the lift.

'I'll meet you down there,' said Rubi.

'I'll come with you,' said Vito.

Dennis and Minnie slid Biggy to the top

of the stairs. Unfortunately, they couldn't see exactly where the stairs started. Before they knew it, the dinner tray had reached its tipping point and they found out what kind of noise an eight-foot-tall, 1,000 lbs snowmenace makes when it rides down eighteen concrete stairs on a shiny metal dinner tray.

WAKKA-WAKKA-WAKKA-WAKKA!

SCREEEEAM!

WAKKA-WAKKA-WAKKA-WAKKA!

HOOOOOWL!

WAKKA-WAKKA-WAKKA-WAKKA!

WAKKA-WAKKA-WAKKA-WAKKA-WAKKA!

SHRIEK!

KERBLAMMO!

WOO-HOO!

. . . GROAN . . .

Biggy was fine. In fact, it had been quite good fun! They made their way to the room with the trapdoor, which led to the tunnels under the school, but the trapdoor was locked!

'Help me!' shouted Dennis, pulling at the handle with all his strength. Minnie grabbed hold of him and pulled too.

'Let our pal do it!' laughed Rubi, when she and Vito arrived. 'It'll be easy for Biggy!'

'Huh! We loosened it for you,' said Minnie, blowing her hair out of her eyes.

Biggy helped Rubi into the tunnel, and the rest jumped down

after them. They made their way through the gloomy, torch-lit tunnels, over an ancient rope bridge and on to the Confiscatorium, where a distant Viking ancestor of Dennis lived in eternal detention. It's not as bad as it sounds – he has a console to pass the time.

'Hi, Viking me!' said Dennis to the Viking boy who was playing FartNite with his Viking dog on the latest console confiscated from a pupil.

'Hi Dennis!' said the Viking boy. 'How's the pillaging and plundering going?'

'We don't really do much of that any more,' said Minnie. 'I don't agree with that personally, but that's the modern world for you.'

'We're in a bit of a rush,' said Dennis. 'Is there a way out of here that won't fire us into the air above the playground on a jet of fizzy cola? We could use a more discreet exit, if you know what I mean.'

Viking Dennis pointed at a door marked "Broom Closet".

'Be my guest,' he said.

In the playground in front of Bash Street School, Mayor Brown and Dr Pfooflepfeffer were on the lookout for the missing snowmenace.

'We've got the school surrounded, Pfooflepfeffer!' he said, standing up. 'That beast is mine.'

'Mine,' corrected Pfooflepfeffer.

'Whatever. Ours,' said the mayor, exasperated. 'As long as we keep our eyes open, there's no way it can get past us!'

Behind them, the gang tiptoed out of the playground onto Bash Street itself. At the end of the street two police cars were parked.

'A road block!' said Dennis. 'What now?'

Biggy grabbed him and tucked him under one of their enormous arms. He sat Vito on one shoulder, then lifted Minnie on to the other. A huge hairy paw was placed firmly on the back of Rubi's chair. Gnasher jumped into Dennis's arms.

'I don't normally let anyone push me around,' Rubi said, 'but I'll make an exception for you.'

Biggy dropped the shiny metal dinner tray onto the snow, put one foot on it and pushed off with the other . . . heading straight for the road block!

'You're going the wrong way!' Vito shouted into Biggy's ear. 'We're supposed to be running away from them, not towards them!'

At the last moment, just when it seemed impossible not to smash into the parked police cars, Biggy kicked down on the back of the tray, and . . .

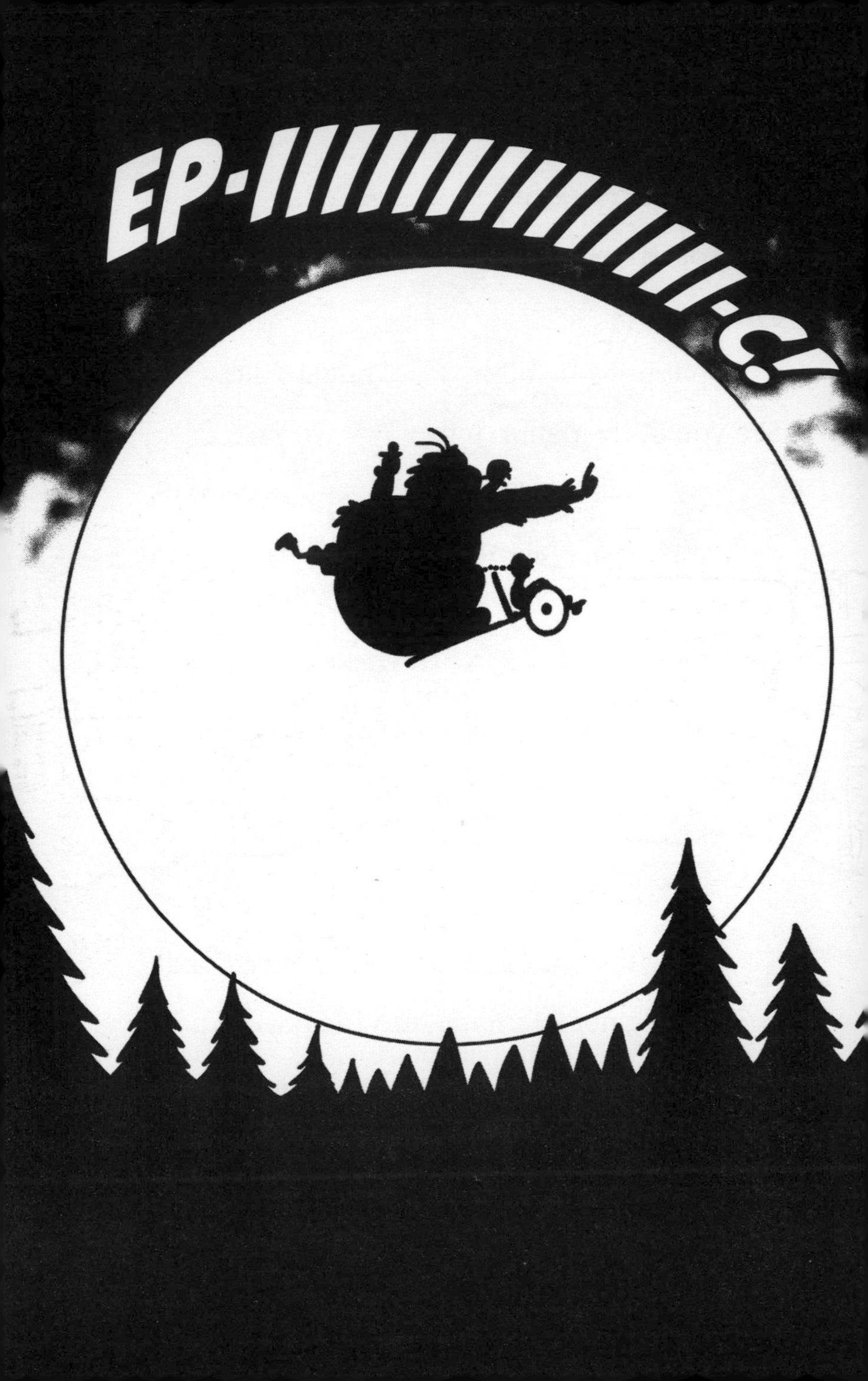
EP-IIIIIIIIIIIIIIII-C!

Biggy nailed the landing and dropped the gang back on solid ground. Well, solid snow. They'd made it!

'Split up!' cried Dennis. 'They'll follow us! See you at the den in ten!'

## Chapter Seven

# WHAT SHALL WE DO WITH THE STINKY SNOWMAN?

Dennis and Gnasher led Biggy Smells back to the den, but first they went to his Gran's house so he could get them some choccy biscuits.

WHAT DID YOU SAY YOUR NEW FRIEND'S NAME WAS?

THIS IS BIGGY, GRAN. BIGGY SMELLS!

He certainly does! Gnee-hee!

'That's nice,' said Gran. 'Hang on, did you say . . .'

But Dennis and his nice-but-niffy new friend were already gone.

When they got to the den, Dennis discovered why Biggy had caused so much damage. His massive mate was just too big to fit inside!

'Why did you squeeze yourself in?' asked Dennis.

Biggy pointed to the sweetie drawer, drooling just a little bit.

'Sweets, eh? There's a Red Hot Chilli Gobstopper left if you want it' Dennis offered.

Biggy frowned and mimed being violently sick. Five times. All over the den.

'Thank goodness you spat it out,' said

Dennis. 'We can fix the den, but there's no way I'm mopping up Bigfoot barf!'

Suddenly . . .

**RAT·A·TAT·TAT·TAT!**

**RAT·TAT·TAT·TAT.**

**RAT·A·TAT·A·TAT·A·TAT.**

**TAT·A·RAT·A·TAT·TAT·TAT!**

*The secret knock,* thought Dennis. *Well, almost.*

'I don't know why Rubi made that secret knock so complicated,' he muttered.

'Try again!' called Dennis through the door. 'You missed a "tat" somewhere in the middle.'

'Shut up and let us in, or I'll practise that stupid secret knock on your forehead!' said a voice that sounded suspiciously like Minnie's.

Dennis looked at Biggy, who shrugged.

Dennis opened the door. In trooped Vito and Minnie. Rubi wheeled herself up the ramp.

'Were you followed?' asked Dennis.

'Of course not!' said Minnie.

Biggy stood up, head bumping on the roof. The den shook.

'Sit down over there,' said Minnie, pointing. 'You'll bring the whole den down!'

'No one puts Biggy in a corner!' said Dennis hotly.

'You two can argue later,' Rubi interrupted. 'Biggy's here now, and they need our help. What are we going to do?'

'I think we should take them back to Mount Beano,' said Vito. 'That's their natural environment and they can keep themselves hidden there.'

'Couldn't we make them a home bit closer to Beanotown?' asked Rubi. 'It would be amazing to find out more about them.'

'That's too risky,' said Minnie. 'The mayor will soon be tearing the woods apart to get his trophy.'

*RAT-A-TAT-TAT-TAT!*
*RAT-TAT-TAT-TAT.*
*RAT-A-TAT-A-TAT-A-TAT.*
*TAT-A-RAT-A-TAT-TAT-TAT!*

'The mayor!' said Vito.

'If it is the mayor, he knows the secret knock better than any of us,' said Dennis, sarcastically. He opened the door.

'Pie Face!' said Rubi.

'Hi!' said Pie Face. 'What happened to the den? Why weren't you in class after break? And why are the mayor and a dozen of his men searching the woods?'

Dennis sighs. 'So many questions! Still, there's an easy answer to all of them . . .'

THAT!

'Oh boy!' said Pie Face to Biggy. 'Are you a Sasquatch?'

Biggy looked blank.

'What's a Sasquatch?' asked Minnie.

'A Sasquatch is like a Bigfoot,' said Pie Face, 'or the Abominable Snowman!'

'Biggy came down from Mount Beano last night,' explained Vito, 'and we don't know what to do to keep them safe from the mayor, Dr Pfooflepfeffer, and whoever else wants to catch them.'

Pie Face nodded. 'Have you asked them what they want to do?'

'Pie Face, you're a genius!' said Dennis.

'Biggy', said Dennis. 'What do **YOU** want to do?'

'It's no use,' said Rubi. 'Biggy can't

understand us, and we can't understand Biggy.'

'Whatever you're going to do,' said Pie Face, 'you have to do it soon, because the mayor and his goons are coming this way!'

Dennis made a decision.

'Rubi, Vito,' said Dennis. 'You take Biggy up Mount Beano. Me, Minnie, Pie Face and Gnasher will run interference down here in the woods to buy you time to get away.'

Rubi and Vito nodded.

'I've got a better idea,' said Minnie. 'We'll do your plan, but say it was my idea all along.'

'Whatever,' said Dennis.

Pie Face kept watch at the door while Rubi and Vito got ready.

'Is the coast clear, Pie Face?' Rubi asked.

'I don't know,' said Pie Face. 'I can't see the coast from here. There's no one outside, though.'

'Good enough,' said Rubi, smiling at Vito.
Pie Face had his own way of thinking.

'You ready, big dude?' Vito asked Biggy.
Biggy grinned. They liked Vito.

'Let's go!' said Rubi, aiming her chair down
the ramp. Vito and Biggy followed, Biggy
bumping their head on the roof again as they
stepped onto the ramp.

Dennis and Minnie watched as their friends
made their way through the woods.

'Okay,' said Dennis. 'Enough of the soppy stuff. Let's get ready!'

## Chapter Eight

# DO YOU WANNA SEE A SNOWMAN?

It felt like the entire, groan-up world was closing in, ready to squish them like a bag of jelly babies, trapped underneath your Super Epic Turbo Cricket kit at the bottom of a battered school bag.

'Everyone okay with the plan?' asked Dennis. 'Good! Let's get to work!'

Using things they had lying around the den, they'd created an abominably **GOOD** costume. Dennis and Pie Face had Minnie sitting on their shoulders. Gnasher was king of the castle, his legs wrapped like a scarf around Minnie's neck.

Gnasher's jaws glinted in the darkness, as if they belonged to the creature itself! Minnie had brushed them, using tomato ketchup, to add to the fear factor. She'd used Dennis's toothbrush, of course. Draped over them all was the ancient, moth-eaten sheepskin rug from the den, smeared with two full pots of Har Har's Joke Shop Slime.

Anyone who spotted them would need a swift trip to the bathroom. It didn't matter who caught up with them first. The army, police or the mayor and his heavies would all be scared off when they spotted the

surprise Minnie had in store for them. Who knew some tennis rackets, an old rug, three kids and a dog could look so bone-chillingly horrid?

Minnie had also laid a fake trail of giant-sized footprints in a wide circle around the den. The idea was to make it look as if the snowmenace was prowling nearby.

They hoped the hunters would be delayed while they followed the footsteps around in circles, and Rubi, Vito and Biggy would get a head start as they headed for Biggy's home.

That's when the second part of their scheme would kick in: to make the pursuers feel as if a peckish, horrible monster was actually hunting THEM . . .

The classic switcheroo, the hunters becoming the hunted!

'About that flan you mentioned?' asked Pie Face. His stomach made a loud, growling rumble.

'I said "plan", Pie Face, not flan,' explained Dennis. 'Plan A was the fake footsteps Minnie made using the tennis rackets. Plan B is your bit – to make another type of racket with Rubi's synthesiser.'

They heard a helicopter overhead. It was now or never.

Pie Face looked confused, which wasn't unusual.

'A sympathiser? I've got no sympathy for the mayor and his heavies!'

'Just think of yourself as the "Pied" Piper

of Beanotown,' said Minnie, 'only instead of following you, we want these rats to run away from your abominable din.'

'An abominable din? I can make that!' said Pie Face, grinning wildly.

The forest surrounding the den was darker than Gnasher's fur. Wilbur and Walter Brown were enjoying the chase, smugly cosy in their warm fluffy coats. The labels promised they were made from 100% abominable snowman fur!

WE KNOW THE BEAST LIKES ICE LOLLIES, SO I'M RODDY FOR ACTION!

I HAVEN'T BEEN SO EXCITED SINCE I BAGGED YOUR PET HAMSTER THAT ESCAPED INTO THE BASEMENT, WALTER!

Walter confidently dangled a fishing rod, baited with a strawberry ice cream lolly in the shape of a foot. Wilbur carried his grandfather's 'fishing kit' – a cruel spear used on whaling expeditions.

They both carried nets, the sort you'd take to the seaside.

'Do you want to catch a snowman?' sang Walter creepily, as his nose started to drip.

He was desperate to catch this monster. It could be worth millions. If it was forced to perform for the rest of its days, or was stuffed as a trophy in father's study, it made no difference to him.

He imagined the noise of the crowds cheering when they returned to town with the beast in their nets.

That's when he spotted the footprints. GIANT footprints. They looked fresh. He stepped into one. **What?!** *Surely the beast* wasn't **THAT humongous?**

'Daddy,' he whispered. 'We're going to need a bigger net!'

His teeth began to chatter – and it was nothing to do with the cold. The howling wind was making the leaves in the tree sound like they were whispering to each other.

Walter realised he was scared. He was even more afraid when he heard his dad – the most powerful man in Beanotown – let out a **blood-curdling**

**SCREAM!**

A fearsome sight had emerged from the

darkness. Twice as tall as Wilbur and three times as wide. It was a horrible sight – the most abominable snowman imaginable. Dirty matted fur, covered with slime, teeth dripping red and vicious claws swiping back and forth, ready to slice its prey to shreds.

'I hope it doesn't like posh food,' sniffed
Walter.

'I hope it doesn't like food with poop in its
pants,' gulped Wilbur.

Looming above the helpless Browns,
Gnasher was enjoying the ride. And he'd been
storing up a particularly evil dog-fart just for
this moment . . .

BBBBBBBBBBBBRRRRRRRRAAAAAAPPPTTT!

To Walter and Wilbur, it sounded like a foul,
inhuman growl.

Although Minnie, Dennis and Pie Face had experienced Gnasher letting rip before, the abominable aroma caused them to topple in a fit of coughs and splutters, into the middle of a deep snowdrift.

As they climbed out of the drift, their makeshift costume flopped to the ground, leaving them shivering and exposed. Instantly they were transformed from terrifying monster into three kids and a soggy, groggy doggy.

Their epic plan to buy their friends time to escape had turned into an epic fail. They shook themselves free of snow and prepared to face the music.

## Chapter Nine

# THE PLAN GOES BLAM!

To the gang's utter amazement, the mayor and his crack team of hunters had scarpered!

'I love it when a plan goes BLAM!' Dennis cheered.

WHEN <u>MY</u> PLAN GOES BLAM, YOU MEAN!

Pie Face thought Dennis had said 'flan' again, so he quickly dropped the post-mission quiche he was scoffing, in case it was about to explode.

The hunters had become the hunted and seemed to have given up their pursuit, for now at least. They'd made sure Biggy Smells had a good head start on their journey back to their home at the summit of Mount Beano.

Now it was time to head back to the den. Walter and his dad had been sent packing, but they might not be the only ones out looking for Biggy Smells.

As they approached the den, they stopped in their tracks.

## DEN . . . DEN . . . DENNN!

A tall figure was clearly standing by the window. Too tall to be any of the gang. Had Walter and Wilbur retreated here?

Suddenly, they heard an angry yell. It was Rubi.

'You've eliminated my friends!'

'Come on,' said Dennis. 'We have to help!'

They burst into the den, ready for one last stand. Their jaws dropped at the scene before them. Rubi, Vito and Biggy Smells were playing a game of FartNite, as if they didn't have a care in the world.

SOMEONE'S IN THE DEN!

'**Wai-what?**' said Minnie. 'We've been out there giving you a head start! Biggy could have been home by now.'

'The Mayor will be back with reinforcements soon,' warned Dennis.

Biggy looked guilty.

Vito launched into a hasty explanation.

'Every time we walked away from the den, Biggy curled up into a ball . . .'

'. . . an abominable snowball . . .' interrupted Rubi.

'. . . then rolled straight back down to the den,' finished Vito.

'Then they cuddled us so tightly, I nearly pumped,' said Rubi. 'They wanted to stay here, with us, not go back to the mountain.'

'OK, brainbox,' challenged Minnie. 'What do we do now?'

She was staring straight at Rubi. The pals always turned to Rubi when they'd run out of crazy ideas, as she usually came up with a really smart one.

'The more brainwaves, the better,' Rubi said. 'Let's see if the Group Chat has any suggestions.'

Rubi typed a message on her tablet. She made it sound like the start of a joke so any adults who saw it wouldn't be suspicious.

**Rubi:** How do you get an abominable snowman to do what you want?

The first answer flashed up almost immediately. It was from Betty. Rubi's heart sank when she read the message.

**Betty:** Simples! Ask it nicely!

**Rubi:** Thx, Betty.  We'll try that. Anyone else?

**Calamity James:** Ask them to toss a coin. Heads, they do what you want, tails they do what they want. Knowing my luck, they'll want to eat me.

**Roger:** Just let them stay in the den and tell anyone who comes snooping that Gnasher's dad is visiting.

SO MUCH FOR US ALL PUTTING OUR BRAINS TOGETHER. I THINK THIS WEATHER HAS CAUSED A BEANOTOWN BRAIN FREEZE.

I AGREE. WHATEVER WE DECIDE, WE'RE STUCK HERE FOR THE MOMENT. LET'S JUST CHILL OUT FOR A BIT.

Biggy yawned.

'What about a bedtime story?' Rubi asked. 'Dennis, you read one to Bea every night, don't you?'

Biggy looked confused. Dennis held up a copy of *The Battle for Bash Street School*. Biggy smiled and nodded.

Dennis began to read.

The friends all listened quietly. Dennis was good at telling stories. Soon there was a contented SIGH, and Biggy started to snore. LOUDLY! And then, a new sound, louder than the snoring. The friends looked at each other. A shiver ran down Vito's spine.

## KNOCK!

## KNOCK!

## KNOCK!

Someone, or some*thing*, was at the door.

## Chapter Ten

# BABY BIGGY

Dennis slowly opened the door.

Snow swirled into the den. There was nothing there. Was it just their imaginations?

Suddenly, something tickled his tummy! A small, furry, hand. Dennis jumped so high, he almost left his shorts behind.

Right under his nose, standing patiently on the doorstep, was a cute, baby Biggy.

Or so he thought.

BABY SMELLS?

'Are you going to invite me in, guys? I'm about to freeze solid.'

It was Betty! She was wearing a furry snowsuit and balaclava which made her look like Biggy's baby sister!

Before they could ask what she was doing here, Betty explained that if they were having trouble with an abominable snowman, then she was the best person to help. 'First, never call an abominable snowman "abominable",' she started. 'They hate that. Second, never call an abominable snowman a "snowman". The correct word is yeti.'

The pals gawped at her in amazement. Biggy sat up and yawned.

'I'm from Nepal, remember,' said Betty. 'And so are yetis.'

Betty turned to Biggy and said, नमस्कार *

Biggy smiled, lumbered over and padded a gentle high five on Betty's mitten. Then

*This is how you say 'Hello' in Nepali – the language of Nepal. I had to learn it for this part of the book. It's easier than Gnasherese, but I'll translate back into English from here on. – clever Ed.

they launched into a deep conversation in Nepali. None of the gang could understand a word.

When they had finished, Betty translated Biggy's story for the rest of the gang.

'The yeti was born on Mount Everest, in the Himalayas.

They lived there happily for years. Then more and more climbers came, leaving litter and even poo lying on the sacred slopes of their homeland.'

So our friend here decided to explore the world in search of a new home with snow as nice as Mount Everest's. After wandering for many years, the yeti found Mount Beano. It's nice and cold at the top, the snow is Superior Snow, and there are always lots of funny things happening in the town below.'

Biggy chuckled.

WELL, THEY LOOKED LIKE NICE CHILLY MOUNTAINS FROM A DISTANCE! I WANT MY MUMMY!

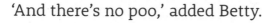

'And there's no poo,' added Betty.

'Poor Biggy was driven away from his home,' said Vito. 'What a shame!'

'It could be worse,' said Dennis. 'Biggy could have ended up in Dandytown . . .'

Everyone laughed. Biggy joined in with a deep throaty chuckle, then growled something else to Betty.

'Biggy has lived alone at the summit of Mount Beano ever since,' she said. 'When the snow came last night, it was only natural for a yeti to go exploring. Then you came along and tracked them down at the school. Today has been the most fun Biggy's had since leaving Mount Everest.'

PAT

PAT

IT'S NICE THAT BIGGY FITS IN. EVEN IF HE DOESN'T ACTUALLY FIT IN . . .

'What now, Biggy?' asked Dennis.

Yeti and Betty conferred once again.

'Biggy wants to stay here with us,' she said. 'Yetis need friends too. Biggy is tired of hiding and being alone.'

'Well,' said Dennis. 'As far as I'm concerned, everyone is welcome in Beanotown, no matter where they come from.'

Biggy whispered in Betty's ear. Betty nodded.

'There's one more thing,' added Betty. 'Biggy is actually a boy, but they quite like it when you talk about them as "they".'

'There's only one teensy problem,' Minnie said. 'If Biggy doesn't want to hide, how do we stop the mayor from finding them?'

## Chapter Eleven

# YETI FOR HIRE

'Maybe, we don't have to hide them at all,' said Dennis excitedly.

Rubi gave him a funny look. Biggy was public enemy number one. Army helicopters were still buzzing about like angry wasps, looking for them!

'There are bizarre, gigantic creatures everywhere in Beanotown,' said Dennis. He started to list them, to prove his point:

YOU MAY TURN THE PAGE... NOW

'But that's just normal people in fancy dress trying to sell stuff,' snorted Minnie.

'So what?' said Dennis. 'If Biggy can get a job like that, they could hang out in Beanotown full-time, without anyone suspecting a thing. Thanks to our prank, the mayor has no idea what the real Biggy looks like!'

Rubi laughed and showed them all her tablet. 'Mayor Brown told the Beanotown Bugle that the monster he escaped from was the size

of a house, oozed toxic slime and even had a fearsome six-pack. The headline was ATTACK OF THE ABDOMINAL SNOWMAN!'

'Biggy can live in the den, can't they?' said Pie Face. 'How would anyone find out?'

'Maybe the smell?' said Minnie. From anyone else that would have sounded unkind, but Minnie was just being honest. Biggy needed a bath.

Pie Face replied, 'My dad's Terry Tortoise, and he smells a lot worse than Biggy when he peels off his shell suit. But after a quick spray of Stynx body spray, he's good to go.'

Rubi had an idea.

'It would be loads easier for Biggy if they didn't need you to translate for them, Betty. Maybe I could invent a gadget that converts everything they say into English.'

'That would be amazeballs,' said Dennis.

'Can you make one for Gnasher too?'

'Only if he speaks Nepali,' said Rubi.

Gnasher wasn't impressed. *I'll just stick to farting, barking, howling and growling, ta very much.*

'Never mind,' said Dennis. 'I can read him like a book anyway. And speaking of books, Biggy won't let go of that story I read to them.'

Biggy mumbled, cuddling the book protectively as if it was a teddy bear. Betty listened to them carefully.

'Biggy can understand us all really well,' she said. 'Nepali is the only human language that yetis can speak, but what they're really good at is listening. A good listener is a wise friend.'

Biggy cleared his throat. The gang listened

for whatever wisdom Biggy would share next.
It was the quietest the den had ever been.
The silence was broken when Biggy shared a
humongous yeti fart.

BETTER OUT THAN IN!
SHARING'S CARING...

PHWARP!

'That's settled,
then,' said
Dennis. 'Biggy
needs a job
where people
will assume they're
talking to a yeti who is
actually a human being
dressed as a yeti. Simples!'

'Easy as pie,' grumbled a doubtful
Minnie. Pie Face looked up, crossing first his
fingers, then his arms and legs, in hope of an
unexpected feast.

'You look a bit cross, Pie Face,' joked Rubi, playfully.

'There are loads of places that need help attracting people,' said Dennis. 'A yeti mascot would have the crowds flocking in!'

'A place where listening is important would love Biggy,' said Vito.

'True,' said Rubi, 'but it also needs to be chilly. If the job is serving grub in a steamy chip van, Biggy will be chucking chip butties at the customers!'

'I'd pay extra to see that,' said Minnie, trying to be helpful.

'What about the library?' asked Pie Face. 'It must be cold in there, because all the books have jackets.'

'Ha! They have loads of books about Bigfoot too,' joked Vito, 'in the "large-print" section!'

'The school library needs an assistant librarian,' said Rubi. 'Mrs Binding said the last guy quit after a a full set of Harry Snotter books fell on his head.'

'He only had his shelf to blame!' chuckled Dennis.

Mrs Binding is the chief librarian in Beanotown. She's in charge of Beanotown Library and the library at Bash Street School. There are 25,000 books, 4100 magazines and 32 cheese plants under her care. Oh, and a ghost librarian.

I'll tell you about her in another story – Ed.

'Mrs Binding would do anything to get more kids to realise that reading's fun,' said Rubi. 'Having a mascot as assistant librarian would really help her. Check out the yeti, then check out a book.'

'That's clever,' said Vito. 'But so is Mrs Binding, and she's already thought of it – I saw an advert in the *Beanotown Bugle* the other day. "Library Mascot Wanted. No bookworms. Must like stamping."'

Biggy laid their copy of *The Battle for Bash Street* on the table and mimed stamping it with its return date.

The table collapsed beneath their massive paw. Everyone laughed. Biggy was going to be the coolest librarian in history.

## Chapter Twelve

# A CYCLOPS, A YETI AND A UNICORN WALK INTO A LIBRARY . . .

There were two other candidates for the job. Mrs Binding had asked them all to come to the library so she could interview them.

'Biggy will **CRUSH** it,' said Betty, meaning their pal's job interview.

THEY MIGHT CRUSH MRS BINDING!

Rubi was super confident. 'Biggy's a librarian, mascot, PR and advertising campaign all rolled into one. What could be more perfect?'

Biggy's competitors were also dressed as mythical creatures. There was a unicorn and a cyclops.

'That's an accident waiting to happen,' Dennis muttered to Minnie as they waited for the interview to start. 'One wrong move and that poor cyclops won't be reading anything for a while!'

Dennis was right.

There was a Beano lying on the table in front of the cyclops and the unicorn. Dennis watched as they both eyed it, neither wanting to seem selfish by taking the only comic for themselves. Then they both leaned forward at the same time to pick it up, and the unicorn's horn jabbed the cyclops in the eye.

'Ooh! That's gotta hurt!' said Minnie, wincing.

The unicorn was distraught and fussed over the cyclops, who held his only eye.

'I feel so guilty!' said the unicorn. 'Your eye's all bloodshot!'

'Don't worry, it's not my real eye,' said the cyclops. 'Although it does hurt, weirdly.'

The cyclops went home to bathe his fake eye, and the unicorn went with him, to make sure he got there safely. Biggy was the only candidate left!

Mrs Binding called Biggy in for the interview. She looked them up and down . . . and smiled.

'I like your thinking, Mr Smells. Read yeti-nother book!

Genius, and your costume is so realistic,' she said. 'Kids will adore it.'

Biggy felt a tiny bit guilty, but just nodded and smiled. Mrs Binding poured them both a cup of tea and started the interview. She never did anything without a fresh cup of tea.

First, Biggy had to do a short presentation on why they were the best candidate for the job. Rubi had set up some slides on her tablet.

I CAN DO THIS JOB STANDING ON ONE LEG...

Biggy flicked through them as Mrs Binding

sipped her

tea, nodded

and smiled. Result.

Next was the practical

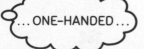

...ONE-HANDED...

...SITTING DOWN...

test. Biggy had to retrieve a heavy book from the furthest, highest shelf in the library as quickly as possible. The fact Biggy had climbed Mount Everest meant this was easy-peasy.

The final part would be trickier – answering any questions Mrs Binding may have. Luckily, Dennis had thought of this already, and had coached Biggy to give Mrs Binding the idea that any question could be answered wordlessly. Perfect in a library!

Mrs Binding held Biggy's application letter, which had been typed by Vito.

'So, Biggy Smells. It says here you were born at a very young age?'

...IN MY SLEEP!

Biggy nodded furiously. It was true!

'And you're something of a whizz kid, genius and Nobel prize winner?'

Yeti blushed strongly, cheeks glowing pink. Mrs Binding liked modesty in her employees.

'I see you don't want to be boastful. I like that. Do you possess any unique skills?'

Biggy began to panic. This was a difficult question to answer without speaking. Their next move was all or nothing. They lifted Mrs Binding's posh china teapot from the table and blew into the spout. The lid hovered, like a flying saucer and . . .

IF THIS DOESN'T MAKE ME HER CUP OF TEA, NOTHING WILL.

Biggy had invented the fastest, most spectacular pour since tea had arrived in Beanotown! Mrs Binding beamed.

'Bravo! How absolutely tea-lightful!'

She then stared directly at Biggy. 'My final, most important question, is this: truly, why do you want this job?'

Biggy held a massive furry finger to massive furry lips and said . . .

And, with a wink and a smile, Biggy was done.

'Well,' Mrs Binding whispered, 'we don't often do that nowadays, but it's lovely to meet someone who understands the old ways.

You've got the job.'

Mrs Binding was delighted with her new
team member, and the library
had never been so busy.

Kids were queuing up to have their books
stamped out by Biggy.

'Is my book due back?' they would ask,
desperate to see that shaggy face smile and

give a nod or a shake of the head.

Biggy loved the library because of all the amazing stories waiting to be read, and Dennis and friends could come and visit every day.

The den was Biggy's new home. Betty and Biggy were like best friends, and Biggy treated Betty like a little sister. She even invited Biggy to stay at her house in the holidays. Her parents couldn't know Biggy was there, of course, but by then the yeti was so good at being quiet there was never any chance of that.

Beanotown Library had never had it so good. Even the Prime Minister begged Mrs Binding to let him visit so he could understand why kids in Beanotown were reading more books than anywhere else in the whole world.

Soon, other Beanotown companies started

trying to headhunt Biggy to work for them instead of the library.

Betty explained to Biggy that a headhunter is someone who tries to get people to work for their company, not the type of person a rare yeti would have to hide from.

Biggy turned down every offer, because the job at the library was just perfect.

Then, one day, someone made Biggy an offer they couldn't refuse . . .

# Chapter Thirteen

# TAKING NO CHANCES

WARNING THIS CHAPTER MAY CONTAIN BAD LUCK!

Good point, James! Let's just move on to the next chapter! – careful Ed.

## Chapter Fourteen

# THE FART
# OF THE DEAL

At the Town Hall, Mayor Brown has installed a private elevator for him and ... well, just him, actually.

THE
BROWN
ELEVATOR
(PRIVATE)

The offer Biggy couldn't refuse came from the one person who might actually want to hunt Biggy's head and hang it on his wall: Mayor Wilbur Brown.

When the Mayor first contacted Mrs Binding, she suspected he wanted to hire Biggy as a mascot for WilburCorp. She was right.

Wilbur had always used himself as the face of his company, but was now jealous of how popular the library's larger-than-life mascot had become. He wanted WilburCorp to have a slice of the yeti action.

Mrs Binding didn't want Biggy to leave the library, but she thought it was only fair for Biggy to hear what the mayor was offering.

Mayor Brown arrived at the library clutching an expensive-looking leather briefcase. When he popped it open, a flask of coffee and some smoked salmon sandwiches fell out.

'That's a fancy packed lunch box,' said Betty, who was there to act as Biggy's agent.*

*You know, like a Premier League footballer's agent – Ed.

Mayor Brown sneered at Betty and explained he didn't trust food made by people who weren't chefs. Biggy shrugged and tucked into the biscuits Mrs Binding had carefully prepared for their VIP guest.

*Waste not, want not,* thought Biggy.

The yeti burped. Loudly. Wilbur wrinkled his nose as the stink reached his breathing space. It was a farty smell. Betty crossed her fingers that bad manners hadn't given Yeti away.

Wilbur kicked off the meeting by ordering Biggy to take off their mask.

DOES HE THINK I'M A POLO BEAR?!

BURP!

TWO WORDS – "BREATH" AND "MINTS".

'I want to look you in the eye,' he said.

Biggy gulped.

Luckily, Mrs Binding interrupted.

'I don't think so. You'd only try to read the label inside, then order one for yourself online. Why don't you create a mascot of your own? I thought you were coming to deal, not steal?'

Biggy looked worried, but Betty giggled. Mrs Binding was pretty formidable.

Wilbur narrowed his eyes, glaring at Betty and Mrs Binding.

'I need an actor,' he explained, 'to pose for some pictures. I'm creating a **WANTED** poster.'

Wilbur pointed at Biggy and said, 'I want **YOU** to

pretend to be the real, bigger, uglier, scarier, utterly **ABOMINABLE** snowman I discovered in Beanotown Woods a few weeks back.'

'I want everyone to know how amazingly brave I was and that I definitely didn't scream and run away or poop in my hunting britches.'

'Once people understand how horrid and terrifying this abominable snowman is, they'll hunt it down to please their beloved Mayor, and that horrible head will finally be mounted on my study wall where it belongs!'

Wilbur panted, and wiped a little spit from his chin.

'My client is a specialist in dressing as a yeti,' said Betty, '**NOT** a so-called abominable snowman, which by the way is a pretty

offensive term. But,' she smiled, 'they could do what you ask, no problemo . . . for a price!'

'Kids these days! It's all about the money.'

Wilbur growled through gritted teeth, grimly remembering the above-inflation increase in pocket money his sneaky son Walter had negotiated earlier that week. Walter had threatened to tell his mum all about what really happened on Mount Beano.

Betty raised an eyebrow. 'It's not about the money. My client wants creative control.'

Before Wilbur could even finish spluttering at her cheek, Betty started to list Biggy's demands.

'You and Walter will star in the posters

I'M ABOUT TO SHOW WHY PEOPLE SHOULD ALWAYS READ THE SMALL PRINT, READERS . . .

too, to demonstrate your . . . erm, bravery.'

Wilbur tried not to grin. He liked the sound of that!

'We will use special effects to demonstrate the FULL terror of the situation you so bravely faced.'

'Of course,' said Wilbur eagerly. 'The more special, the better!'

'Including ear-shattering wails?'

'Yes please!'

'We'll have to give people an idea of the horrendous stink.'

'Absolutely. 100%.'

'Fine,' said Betty, grinning. 'We have a deal. Sign here. I guarantee these posters will become legendary. I'll have them up all over town by teatime. You could even become an online sensation and become the most famous politician since . . .'

Betty paused to let Wilbur use his imagination. She realised she had him hooked, just like Biggy when they spotted an ice lolly . . .

'My client's fee is ONE MILLION . . . ice lollies!'

Betty knew that would keep Biggy cool for the next five years.

Like many powerful men, the details just weren't important to Wilbur Brown. He just wanted to think he was getting his own way, so he agreed to everything Betty proposed. It never even occurred to him that little Betty Bhu was quite a lot smarter than he assumed she was.

And that was a **BIG** mistake!

IS THAT ENOUGH FOR A WHOLE WEEK'S PACKED LUNCHES?

WE'RE GONNA NEED A BIGGER FREEZER!

After posing for pictures with Biggy in front of a green screen background, Wilbur got ready to leave the library.

Biggy handed him his briefcase. The Mayor rudely declined to shake Biggy's outstretched paw. Biggy was a little offended, but only smirked – the sneaky yeti had eaten the mayor's posh sandwiches when he wasn't looking!

As Wilbur strode away, they could hear him phoning Walter.

FETCH THE STEP LADDER. I NEED TO CLEAR A SPACE ON THE WALL IN MY STUDY ... FOR A TRULY ABOMINABLE TROPHY.

I LOVE IT!

Mrs Binding watched him leave and said what everyone was thinking.

'What a horrid man!'

She walked away, shaking her head.

'This is amazing,' said Betty. 'You've just become the face of the campaign to capture . . . yourself! It's a classic double-bluff. Mayor Brown has accidentally guaranteed that you can live here in Beanotown, unsuspected, happily ever after!'

Back at the den that evening, Betty showed the gang the **WANTED** poster that Wilbur had agreed to let her make.

It. Was. Amazeballs! Everything Betty had pranked him into signing up for.

The Mayor's shocking screams.

# WANTED!

**THE ABDOMINAL BEAST OF MOUNT BEANO**

*FOR CRIMES INCLUDING:*
*MAKING OUR GLORIOUS MAYOR*
*. . . POO HIS PANTS*
*. . . SCREAM LIKE A BABY*
*. . . SQUISH HIS ADORABLE CHILD IN HIS RUSH TO ESCAPE!*

*DO NOT APPROACH THIS CREATURE UNLESS YOU ARE ARMED AND DANGEROUS!*

Him trampling his son into the snow to escape.

The fact he'd **POOPED his pants!**

Betty told the gang that Wilbur had started

tearing the posters down as soon he'd seen them. Unfortunately for him, Rubi had also posted it on WHASSUP, and over a million people had 'liked' it already!

Rubi, checking her tablet, interrupted. 'Actually, make that . . . two million!'

Wilbur's plan to have Biggy's head on his study wall was a distant memory.

Biggy winked and growled mischievously. They had one final surprise to reveal.

Betty translated what Biggy said to her, giggling.

'Remember how the Mayor wanted something abominable for his office? Well, he

THAT WILL DEFINITELY KICK UP A STINK!

got it – Biggy dropped a sneaky yeti fart into his empty briefcase! When Wilbur gets home tonight and opens it . . .'

Vito laughed.

'OMG! Imagine how bad an unleashed Biggy Smells Special will be after eight hours trapped in a briefcase!'

Biggy shifted awkwardly on the beanbag.

'Eeek!' cried Betty. 'No need to imagine it!
Here comes one now!'

'Phee-ew!' said Dennis, holding his nose.

'I guess this all goes to show that for Biggy

Smells, home is where the fart is!'

# THE END. OR IS IT?

# School Academic Diary

Name................................
Class................................
Teacher................................

# MANUAL oF MiSCHIEF!

How to think kid and influence teachers...

## [TOP SECRET!]

### KiDS (and yetis) ONLY!!

# BREAK rules, intelligently

It's easier to follow a rule than to think for yourself.

175

# THE LEGENDARY MANUAL of MISCHIEF CONTINUED!

## OUT-OF SCHOOL MISCHIEF!

The Mischief Never Stops for Bash Street Kids!

PSSST!

✳ ✳ ✳

Even on holiday We get up to all sorts of mischief. I wanted to write down some of the funniest stuff that happened on our abominable adventure, as the latest entry in our Manual of Mischief. There're some new jokes, laughs and pranks, so you can be more Beano, like me and my mates. Remember, these secrets are <u>for</u> kids' eyes only!

So SHUSH! (as Yeti would say!)

TOP SECRET!

-DENNIS

# YETI'S TRICKY ENGLISH LESSON

Betty has been helping Yeti ?
understand even more English, with
? some trick questions!

## How many can you get?

1. What's the longest word in the English language?

2. What letter makes a quarter of a KILO?

3. Which English WOrd is always spelt incorrectly?

4. When were there only 3 vowels?

ANSWERS

1. Smiles, cos there's a 'mile'
between the first and last letters
2. Either K, I, L or O
3. Incorrectly!
4. Before U and I were born

(Turn the book upside-down, or stand on your head!)

# PREDICTABLY *FUNNY!*

Ask your teacher to

> Pick any number between **1** and **500**

and tell them you're going to predict what they'll say and write it down on a piece of paper...

You say

was it **239**?

They say

**NO!**

Then you proudly show them the **NO** you've already written on your piece of paper!!

# YOU SNOOZE, you LOSE...

Sleeping in class has never been the smartest move but you can get away with it, on two conditions:

**1.** You don't **SNORE**

**2.**

Draw two eyes onto a piece of paper and cut them out. Close your own tired eyes and simply lick the back of each paper eye and gently stick them to your closed eyelids.

⚠ DO NOT USE GLUE!! ⚠

# THE MATHLETE

Challenge your teacher, or any grown-up, to answer these silly sums:

**1.** When 1 = banana, 2 = yellow and 3 = apple, What does 4 plus 5 equal?

**2.** If you have two coins, totalling 15p and one of them <u>isn't</u> a 5p, what are the two coins?

**3.** Can you subtract 2 from 11 and make the answer even?

%

x = why?

Now turn the book upside-down or stand on your head to read the answers over there!

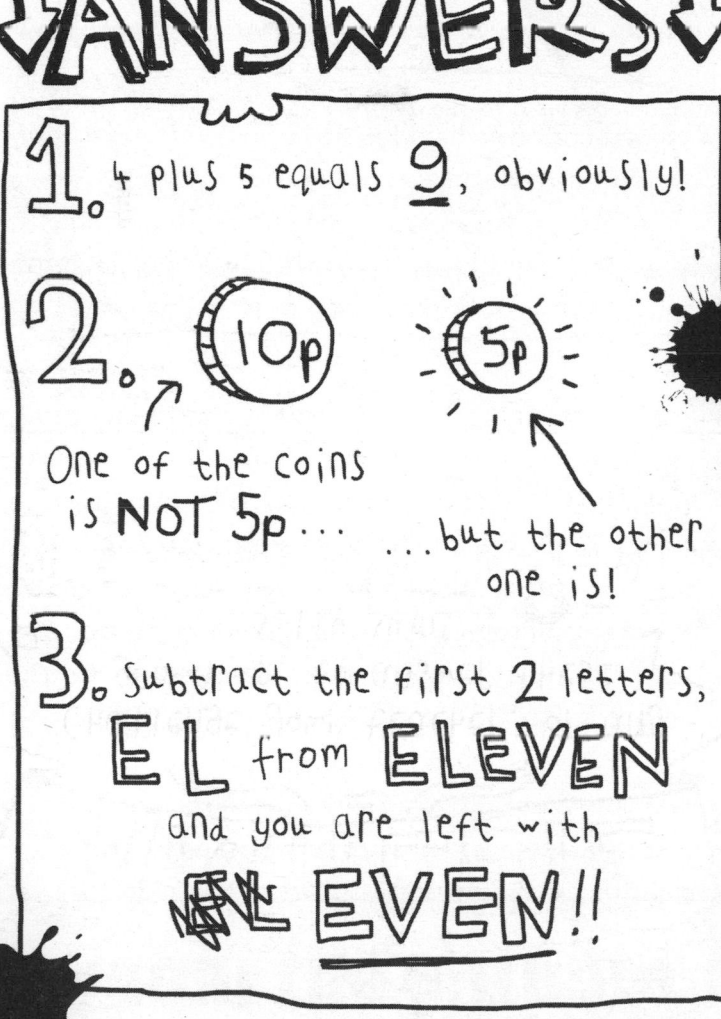

Why did the teacher feel sorry for the maths book? The poor thing had so many problems!

# ↓ANSWERS↓

1. 4 plus 5 equals **9**, obviously!

2. One of the coins is **NOT** 5p... ...but the other one is!

3. Subtract the first 2 letters, **EL** from **ELEVEN** and you are left with **EVEN!!**

# About the Authors

Craig Graham and Mike Stirling were both born in Kirkcaldy, Fife, in the same vintage year when Dennis first became the cover star of Beano. Ever since, they've been training to become the Brains Behind Beano Books (which is mostly making cool stuff for kids from words and funny pictures). They've both been Beano Editors, but now Craig is Managing Editor and Mike is Editorial Director (ooh, fancy!) at Beano Studios. In the evenings they work for I.P. Daley at her Boomix factory, where Craig fetches coffee and doughnuts, and Mike hoses down her personal bathroom once an hour (at least). It's the ultimate Beano mission!

**Craig** lives in Fife with his wife Laura and amazing kids Daisy and Jude. He studied English so this book is smarter than it looks (just like him). Craig is partially sighted, so he bumps into things quite a lot. He couldn't be happier, although fewer bruises would be a bonus.

**Mike** is an International Ambassador for Dundee (where Beano started!) and he lives in Carnoustie, famous for its legendary golf course. Mike has only ever played crazy golf. At home, Mike and his wife Sam relax by untangling the hair of their adorable kids, Jessie and Elliott.

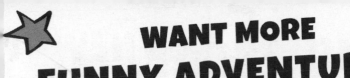

# WANT MORE FUNNY ADVENTURES?

## READ THE BATTLE FOR BASH STREET SCHOOL AND PLAY ALONG WITH THE BOOM-BOX INTERACTIVE STORYBOARD

**BEANO**
**DENNIS & GNASHER**
THE BATTLE FOR BASH STREET SCHOOL

I. P. DALEY
Craig Graham Mike Stirling

illustrated by
Nigel Parkinson

A Beano Studios Product © DC Thomson Ltd (2021)

## READ & PLAY NOW!

**BRING THE ADVENTURE TO LIFE WITH OVER 140 SOUND EFFECTS!**

ZOOM  ♫  CRASH!

PLAY

**PLAY AT BEANO.COM/BOOMIC**

# READ BRAND NEW

# ADVENTURES
## FROM BEANOTOWN